125043

11878
F
DeJ

GEORGE WASHINGTON SCHOOL

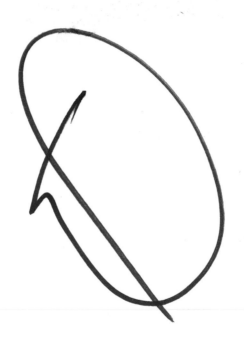

The Happy Birthday Umbrella

the Happy

Little, Brown and Company · *Boston* · *Toro*

Birthday Umbrella

by David Cornel DeJong

Illustrated by Harvey Weiss

An Atlantic Monthly Press Book

For Aunt Helen of Back Bay, Boston

LIBRARY OF CONGRESS CATALOG CARD NO. 59-7342

Second Printing

ATLANTIC-LITTLE, BROWN BOOKS
ARE PUBLISHED BY
LITTLE, BROWN AND COMPANY
IN ASSOCIATION WITH
THE ATLANTIC MONTHLY PRESS

Published simultaneously in Canada
by Little, Brown & Company (Canada) Limited

PRINTED IN THE UNITED STATES OF AMERICA

The Happy Birthday Umbrella

CHAPTER ONE . . . .

ALEXANDER THE GREAT was sitting on the window sill, twitching his black ears and swishing his black tail with the white tip on it.

Young David jumped out of bed and joined Alexander at the window to see what the cat was looking at. It was a large yellow umbrella, lying on the grass, near the curb.

"I think we'd better go out and have a look at that umbrella," said David, and the next moment he and Alexander were on their way downstairs. Neither of them paid any attention to the breakfast sounds that came from the kitchen.

Alexander marched ahead of David down the stairs, and next they were crossing the lawn

together, David on his bare feet. And so they reached the yellow umbrella.

"Oh, it's beautiful," David said to Alexander. "Even if it has no handle, and even if the tip is kind of chewed off."

But Alexander didn't seem to agree with him at all. He sniffed at the umbrella, then touched it carefully with one paw, and last of all he backed away from it as if it were alive.

Alexander didn't want anything to do with the umbrella. He kept backing away from it, turned suddenly, and started running down the little path that crossed the meadow behind the house. A moment later David could see nothing of Alexander except the white tip of his tail bobbing through the tall grass.

Alexander did not like the umbrella.

It was a heavy umbrella, David found out, when he lifted it and started to carry it to the house. In the middle of the lawn he stopped and tried to open it, but it would open only part way. Then it wouldn't close again, and he had to keep carrying it half open.

And it was so large that he couldn't look

around it. He could only hear his father shout
from the door, "David, where did you get that

thing? It must have fallen off a junk truck."

Young David tried to peer past the umbrella at his father, just when Father went hurrying past him. "I've got to hurry and get to work," Father was saying. "You be a good boy now and forget all about that old umbrella and have your breakfast."

Father didn't like the umbrella either.

David was suddenly so hungry that he couldn't think of anything but breakfast. Still hugging the umbrella, he marched toward the kitchen.

"Good morning, Mother," he said, pushing the half-open umbrella ahead of him through the kitchen door.

His mother was feeding the baby. She said, "Happy birthday, David. Your breakfast is

on the table. You're very late, you know."

Mother hadn't seen the umbrella at all. David sat down to his breakfast and set the half-open umbrella beside his chair. Mother still didn't seem to see it. Or perhaps she didn't like it either.

David sighed and tried to feel sad.

Then Mother said, "David, I suppose you've really forgotten that today is your birthday? And that this morning you're going to meet Grandmother at the station when she arrives on the train?"

All at once David felt much better, even if the yellow umbrella had made him forget all about his own birthday and about meeting Grandmother. He knew exactly who would like the umbrella, besides himself. His grandmother would. His grandmother would be sure to like it!

CHAPTER TWO . . . .

AFTER he had eaten his breakfast, and after he'd put on his shirt and pants and jacket and tied his shoes properly, Young David was ready to pick up the umbrella once more to go out and meet his grandmother at the railway station.

He decided to go down the little path across

the meadow. Maybe he'd meet Alexander in the meadow, and perhaps this time Alexander might really like the umbrella.

David didn't see Alexander at all. Not once but three times he stopped and called Alexander's name and waved the umbrella, but nothing happened. He was still so busy looking for Alexander that he reached Joe and Jack's Filling Station at the end of the path before he knew it.

Both Joe and Jack were standing there watching him as he came down the path with his umbrella.

"Davie boy, what's that you're carrying?" Joe asked.

"A yellow umbrella," David said.

"But why don't you open it or close it?" Jack asked.

"It's stuck," David said. "And today is my birthday, and I would like to have it open for my birthday and to meet my grandmother with at the train, and maybe Alexander would like it better too."

"Let's have a look at it," Joe said.

"It's just a little rusty. That's all," Jack said.

Then Joe ran here and Jack ran there, and they came back with a pair of pliers, a can of oil and some sandpaper. They went to work on the yellow umbrella, and a moment later it just flew wide open. It was so large and yellow that David gasped.

When he lifted the open umbrella over his head, he could see nothing of Jack or Joe except the legs of their brown coveralls and their shoes.

"Thank you very much, Jack and Joe," David shouted loudly, as if they couldn't hear him.

"Don't mention it, Davie. It's for your birth-

day," either Jack or Joe said above the umbrella. He didn't know which one.

Then a car pulled up and Jack's and Joe's feet ran off to attend to it. "Just don't get run over under that umbrella, Davie," they shouted.

Once more David peered down the path to see if he could see Alexander the Great. It was much more difficult now, because the big umbrella covered him so completely. But certainly Alexander would be able to see the umbrella now.

Nothing happened. There was nothing to do but to go and meet Grandmother. And maybe if he pretended not to be looking for Alexander, the cat would run up and follow him. That was like Alexander. But nothing at all happened. All he could see as he walked down the sidewalk was

his own feet. But it was very cozy and nice, and
very yellow and private, beneath the umbrella.

CHAPTER THREE.........

Y̶OUNG DAVID could see so little that he had to walk in the middle of the sidewalk. Suddenly somebody said above his yellow umbrella, "What is this? A big umbrella with feet?"

David knew who it was. It was Mr. Bim, the tailor. "It's me!" he shouted. "It's me, Mr. Bim!"

"Well, well, well, if it isn't my friend Young
David, trying to hide himself like a big movie
star," Mr. Bim answered, and kneeled down on
the sidewalk to look up at David beneath the
umbrella.

So, instead of Alexander the Great looking up at him, there was Mr. Bim's face with its small black beard. It looked very funny so close to the sidewalk. "And will you kindly tell me how you can tell where you are going, David?" Mr. Bim was asking him.

"I can't, Mr. Bim," David said. "But I'm going to the station to meet Grandmother because today is my birthday."

"That'll never do. You'll get run over for sure," Mr. Bim said seriously. Then, lifting the umbrella, he marched off with it into his tailor shop.

By the time David caught up with him, Mr. Bim had taken a sharp little knife and had cut four little square windows in the cloth of the umbrella. David sighed, but Mr. Bim didn't seem to be worried at all. Next he put a sheet of clear plastic over each hole and framed each window with black tape. Right there before his own eyes, David saw that his yellow umbrella had gotten four black-framed windows.

Mr. Bim marched up and down his shop beneath the umbrella and said, "Now look, David. See, now I'm looking at you through the front window. And now through the side. And now through the back window."

True enough! Mr. Bim's face with its little black beard appeared at each window in turn.

"Now you can go and meet your grandma and have a happy and safe birthday besides," Mr. Bim said.

"Do they cost a lot? All those windows, Mr. Bim?" David asked before he dared to take the umbrella.

"Well, today is your birthday," Mr. Bim said through a little window. "And that means it won't cost you a cent, Davie."

"Oh, thank you very much, Mr. Bim," David cried. "And now I'd better go and meet Grandmother."

Mr. Bim lifted the umbrella over David's head instead of his own and smiled, "Well, good luck, Davie."

When David marched down the sidewalk again, he stopped to look through the back window of his umbrella. Mr. Bim was in front of his shop waving at him. David waved his own hand behind the little window and then he saw Mr. Bim grinning.

But nowhere did he see any sign of Alexander the Great. Of course, Alexander didn't like the busy street very much anyway. Through the windows of his umbrella David himself could now see all the street and the railway station at the end of it. Why, even Alexander would be safe now beneath the umbrella.

CHAPTER FOUR . . . .

THROUGH the front window of his umbrella, Young David could see Sam sitting in front of his second-hand shop. As he came closer, Sam called, "Oh but I know those blue pants. But never, never before did I see them traveling in a yellow buggy with windows."

David laughed out loud.

"But of course, it's my noble friend Young David. And he's traveling in real style today," Sam cried. "But David, my lad, why do you carry that thing so low?"

"Because the handle is broken off, Sam," David said.

"And the tip looks as if a camel chewed it off," Sam grumbled. "That will never do. Not when you have to travel in style."

This time Sam lifted the umbrella off David's head. He closed it and marched into his store with it. "Now we'll see what we can do for it!" he shouted from his crowded old shop, while David waited outside on Sam's red chair. A little later Sam came out again, looking very dusty.

The thing Sam had in his hand was wonderful to see. It looked like a bird with a long neck which had a knot in it. It had a yellow bill, an orange neck and green eyes. And it certainly was something Alexander would like.

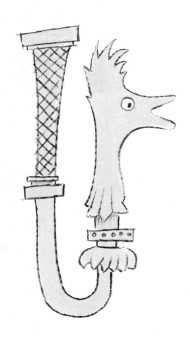

"I'm sure it came off a circus wagon," Sam said. "It's a flamingo, but it fits perfectly. It makes a fine handle."

And Sam screwed the neck of the bird right onto the broken handle. "Oh, it's wonderful," David cried.

"It's a work of art," Sam said. "And it's a flamingo. And just look how high you can hold your umbrella now by the flamingo neck. But we'll make it even better." And from his pocket Sam took a bright red blinker and clamped it over the chewed-off tip of the umbrella. The blinker glittered in the sun.

Sam looked as pleased with the umbrella as David himself. "Also, it's a gift. It's a birthday gift to you, David."

"But I never told you it's my birthday, Sam," David gasped.

"So what? You just happen to look like a boy with a birthday, that's all," Sam laughed.

For quite a little while David couldn't say anything. Everybody was so good to him. Then he shouted, "Thank you very much, Sam! And now I must meet Grandmother."

"That's fine, my boy," Sam said. "Now just let me see you march away, now that you can hold your umbrella good and high. Just hold it high by its flamingo head."

It worked wonderfully. While Sam kept chuckling behind him, David marched on to the station. In his hands curved the beautiful flamingo head. The whole world looked wonderful through the four little windows. Away up top, he just knew, even if he couldn't see it, the blinker must be glittering in the sun. If only Alexander could see him now.

CHAPTER FIVE . . . .

BEFORE he could reach the railway station, Young David thought, the big trouble was that he would have to pass Mrs. Twill's house. Mrs. Twill would be sure to stop him and ask him a hundred or more questions.

Mrs. Twill lived in a house with roses and ivy all over it, just across the street from the station. Mrs. Twill was a baby sitter and knew all about every boy and girl in town.

David tried to walk very quietly past her house, beneath the big yellow umbrella, but of course Mrs. Twill saw him. "David, those are your legs and your feet beneath that great big beautiful umbrella with all the windows in it!" she shouted. "So you come right here on my porch and tell me all about it!"

"But Grandmother's coming off the train, Mrs. Twill."

"The train isn't due for a long time, David. And I know that today is your birthday, and that's why your grandmother is coming. Now come

right here on my porch and I'll give you a lovely
birthday present."

"Can't I come back later, Mrs. Twill?" David
asked.

"Oh no, young man. You sit right down on my porch and I'll fix your birthday present. Why, I have an inspiration."

David sat down, wondering what an inspiration was. It seemed to be a big roll of purple fringe which Mrs. Twill pulled from her sewing basket. "Now just watch," she said, and she started stitching the purple fringe all around the yellow umbrella, while he kept sitting beneath it.

Mrs. Twill stitched and stitched and talked and talked. She wanted to know all about the umbrella, but she talked so much that she didn't even wait for David to tell her. And he wanted to tell her particularly about Alexander the Great, because she knew Alexander, but he got no chance at all.

"Haha!" Mrs. Twill shouted next. "Only ten more stitches to go and it'll be all done."

But at that same moment the train whistle tooted. Grandmother's train was pulling into the station.

David jumped up with his umbrella and went hustling down the porch steps. But Mrs. Twill came running right along with him, stitching and giggling and chattering away, halfway across the street to the railway station. "There, we did it. We finished it," she chattered. "Oh, it's twice as beautiful! Now you run along and meet your grandmother with it."

"Thank you, Mrs. Twill!" David shouted, and kept running. He didn't dare to take the time to look back at Mrs. Twill through the rear window

of his umbrella. He was running so fast that the big umbrella nearly lifted him off his feet, and he was almost sailing toward the station.

CHAPTER SIX . . . .

YOUNG DAVID reached the train platform just in time to see his grandmother step off the train.

Grandmother stood peering around her to see if anyone had come to meet her. But she could not see him, because he had lowered the yellow umbrella so that he could watch her through a little window. She was going to walk right past him when he said, "Good morning, Grandmother," and it was wonderful to see her jump and look and stop.

She dropped all her bundles and cried, "Is that you, David, beneath that yellow umbrella with windows and purple fringes?"

He lifted the umbrella high by its wonderful flamingo head, and Grandmother was under it. "Why, it is the nicest way I have ever been met at the train in all my life." And she hugged him.

Then David had to tell her all about the umbrella, and how everything on it was a birthday present, but that Alexander the Great hadn't liked it at all. But Grandmother just laughed and

said, "Oh, Alexander will. Wait till he sees it now. And I tell you what we'll do now, David. We'll take the path through the fields, and we'll have a fine old time under the umbrella."

They started out at once, and they were having

a wonderful time trotting away together beneath the umbrella and past green grass and white daisies when Grandmother came to a stop and cried, "Oh David, what a goose I am. Why, even Alexander has ten times more sense than I have.

Let's sit right down in the grass here," she said
then. "And let's open that parcel. Why, David,
the very last minute I tucked something in there
for your birthday. Something extra. And I may
as well join everybody else and start celebrating
right away."

While they sat down under the umbrella, Grandmother opened the package and pulled out a small box with silver bells in it. "Do you see what I mean, David? Exactly ten little silver bells, one for each of the ten spokes of your umbrella. And each bell has a little hook on it, and so, presto!"

"Wow!" David shouted, as Grandmother hooked the little bells to the spokes of the great umbrella. "Presto!"

"And when I packed them," Grandmother said, "I asked myself, but what will poor David do with Christmas bells in June? And now look, here we have Christmas in June and your birthday in June, what with this wonderful umbrella."

When they hopped up and started walking again, the great umbrella tinkled as merrily as a Japanese merry-go-round. He and even Grandmother hopped and skipped together up and down the path to make the silver bells tinkle louder. They were in no hurry to get home at all.

They were so happy beneath the yellow umbrella that neither David nor Grandmother noticed that the sun had disappeared behind a black cloud. From that cloud rain began pouring so hard that it jangled and tinkled all the little bells. But they themselves were snug and dry beneath the umbrella, in the middle of a meadow.

And suddenly something black came rushing through the green grass and white daisies and landed right between their feet. It was Alexander

the Great, and he looked so round-eyed and
pleased with himself and the umbrella, and
rubbed his black head so hard against their
ankles, that they had to stop. They laughed so

hard that all the little bells jangled with their laughter. Alexander seemed to like that even better.

"Look, Grandmother, look, he likes my umbrella! He likes it, he likes it!" David shouted. He picked up his cat so that Alexander could get acquainted properly with the lovely flamingo head also.

Alexander rubbed his cheeks against the flamingo head and purred loudly.

It kept raining, but all three, Alexander in the middle, marched safe and dry across the meadow toward home. All the bells tinkled and Alexander purred, and suddenly Grandmother started singing: "Happy birthday to you. Happy birthday to you."

At that very same moment, just when they reached the house, the door burst open, and there was Mother, and then even Father. Mother was carrying a birthday cake with all the candles on it lighted, and the next moment both Father and Mother were under the big umbrella too, with the cake, and both of them joined Grandmother singing: "Happy birthday, dear David. Happy birthday to you."